Touring Motorcycles

JACK DAVID

TM

Are you ready to take it to the extreme?
Torque books thrust you into the action-packed
world of sports, vehicles, and adventure. These books
may include dirt, smoke, fire, and dangerous stunts.
WARNING: read at your own risk.

Library of Congress Cataloging-in-Publication Data

David, Jack, 1968-
  Touring motorcycles / by Jack David.
      p. cm. -- (Torque. Motorcycles)
  Includes bibliographical references and index.
  ISBN-13: 978-1-60014-136-2 (hbk. : alk. paper)
  ISBN-10: 1-60014-136-6 (hbk. : alk. paper)
  1. Motorcycles--Juvenile literature. 2. Motorcycle touring--Juvenile literature. I. Title.

TL440.15.D363 2008
629.227'5--dc22

                                                              2007014200

This edition first published in 2008 by Bellwether Media.

CONTENTS

TOURING MOTORCYCLES IN ACTION

A group of touring motorcycles hum quietly as they glide down the open highway. They are packed with supplies for a two-week journey.

FAST FACT

THE ENGINES OF TOURING MOTORCYCLES PRODUCE A LOT OF TORQUE. THIS IS A VEHICLE'S PULLING POWER. TOURING MOTORCYCLES NEED TORQUE TO CARRY HEAVY LOADS AND PULL TRAILERS.

The riders sit relaxed in their comfortable seats. They are almost through the Great Plains and into the mountains. One of the riders turns up the music on his radio. Their long trip is off to a great start.

WHAT IS A TOURING MOTORCYCLE?

Touring motorcycles are built for long trips. They give a smooth and quiet ride. They can carry one or two riders and even pull a trailer. Touring motorcycles are sometimes also called "dressers" because they can carry so much.

Riders can choose from several types of touring motorcycles. Classic touring motorcycles provide riders with the most storage space. An example of the classic touring motorcycle is the Honda Gold Wing.

Sport touring bikes combine features of touring motorcycles with faster, sleeker **sport bikes**. The Kawasaki Concours 14 is a popular sport touring bike. A third type of touring motorcycle is the touring cruiser. Touring cruisers combine the style of a cruiser with the comfort of a touring bike. Victory makes some of the most popular touring cruisers.

13

FEATURES

Touring motorcycles have lots of storage space in **saddlebags** and trunk compartments. Their seats are soft and comfortable. Most models have radios or CD players and **cruise control** to set the bike's speed.

FAST FACT

THE LONGEST TOUR ON A MOTORCYCLE COVERED 101,322 MILES (163,061 KILOMETERS) AND 50 DIFFERENT COUNTRIES.

Touring motorcycles are perfectly suited for the highway. They have **fairings** to reduce the amount of wind that hits the rider. Touring motorcycles also have powerful engines. Motorcycle engines are measured in cubic centimeters (cc). Most touring motorcycles have engines of 1,000cc. The big engines can pull heavy loads and keep up with cars.

THE TOURING MOTORCYCLE EXPERIENCE

Touring motorcycle owners love long road trips. Riders have room for all of their supplies. They can sit in their comfortable seats for hours.

Touring motorcycles aren't as fast or flashy as other motorcycles. They are designed to be reliable for long distances.

FAST FACT
BMW INTRODUCED THE FIRST TRUE FACTORY TOURING MOTORCYCLE IN THE LATE 1970s. IT WAS CALLED THE R100RT.

Riders drive touring motorcycles differently than most bikes. They don't lean into turns like riders on smaller bikes. They try to stay on paved roads. The heavy bikes aren't suited for off-road riding. For many riders, nothing beats the freedom of the open road.

GLOSSARY

cruise control–a feature that allows a motorcycle rider to maintain a constant speed without holding the throttle

fairing–the drag reducing front panel of a motorcycle

saddlebag–a storage compartment that can be put on the back of a motorcycle

sport bike–a type of motorcycle built for speed and performance instead of comfort

TO LEARN MORE

AT THE LIBRARY

Armentrout, David and Patricia Armentrout.
Touring Bikes. Vero Beach, Fla.: Rourke Pub., 2006.

David, Jack. *Cruisers*. Minneapolis, Minn.: Bellwether, 2008.

Hill, Lee Sullivan. *Motorcycles*. Minneapolis , Minn.: Lerner Publications Co., 2004.

ON THE WEB

Learning more about motorcycles
 is as easy as 1, 2, 3.

1. Go to www.factsurfer.com

2. Enter "motorcycles" into search box.

3. Click the "Surf" button and you will see a list of related web sites.

With factsurfer.com, finding more information is just a click away.

INDEX

The photographs in this book are reproduced through the courtesy of: Kawasaki Motors Corporation, cover, pp. 1, 9, 12-13; Lisa C. McDonald, pp. 4-5; Polaris Industries, pp. 6, 16, 19; BMW Motorrad USA, pp. 7, 17; Graham Prentice, pp. 10-11; Yamaha Motor Corporation, pp. 14-15, 20; Carlos Davila/Getty Images, p. 21.